Rachel Bright & Debi Gliori

Side by Side

ORCHARD

Deep in the heart of Wintermouse Wood,

Down in the grass where the autumn trees stood,

Lived all kinds of creatures – some big and some small –

Some spiky, some furry, some short and some tall.

And here was a family of mouserly folk,

Who nestled in burrow-holes under an oak.

And the tiniest, weeniest, youngest of those,

Who had sticky-out ears and a whiskerly nose,

Was named Little Mouseling – she had a huge heart.

She loved times together . . . not ever apart.

But being so small she was SOMETIMES left out

When her brothers and sisters went up and about.

She would scurry and skip as quick as she could,

But they scattered so fast across Wintermouse Wood.

"Wait for me!" she would sing. "Don't run – oh! Don't hide!

Is there nobody here who will stay by my side?"

Well, in Wintermouse Wood, you don't have to wait long . . .

. . . for one or another to answer your song.

"I'll stay by your side!
Be a friend when you need!"
came the voice of Toad Flip,
who was down in the reeds.

"We could bounce up and down
and do backfloppy jumps,
then plop in the water
and cool down our rumps!"

"How lovely," she said,
for she longed to dive in.
"I do like to bounce
but . . .
THIS mouseling
can't swim."

From high in the branches, a voice echoed down.

"Well, then I'll be your friend!"

bellowed Big Squirrel Brown.

"We can pack up a picnic of hazelnut pie!

... go UP side by side – till we're touching the sky!"

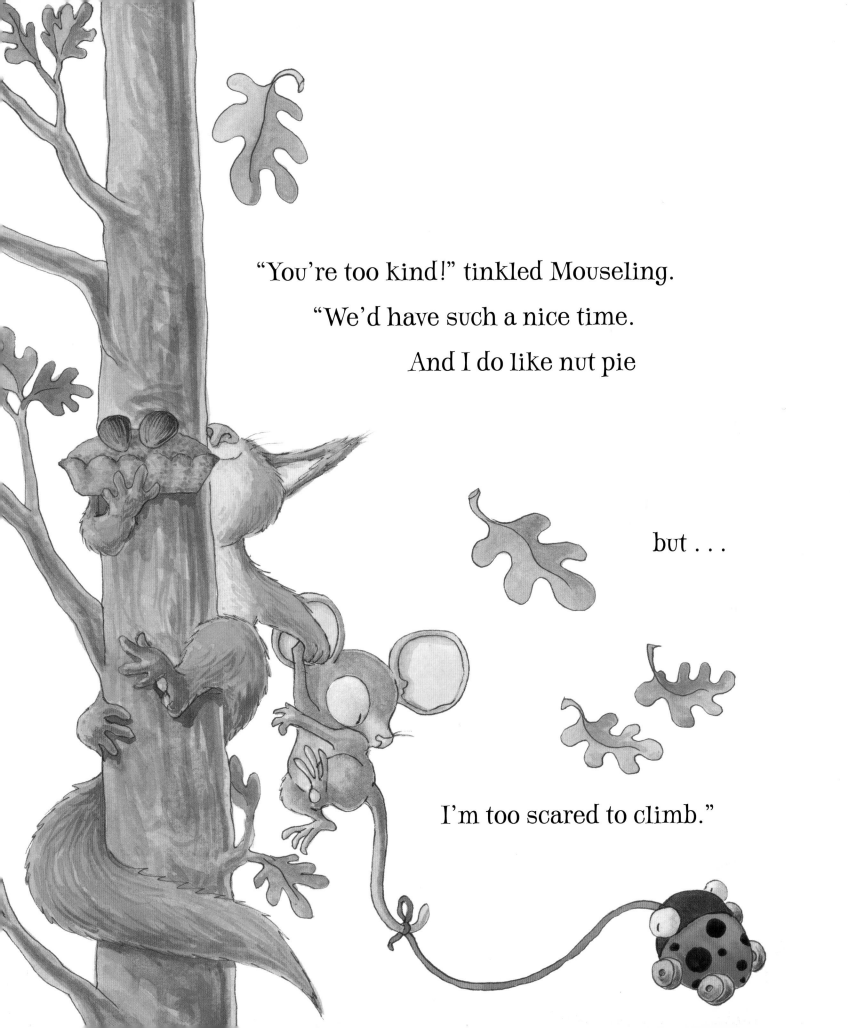

"You're too kind!" tinkled Mouseling.

"We'd have such a nice time.

And I do like nut pie

but . . .

I'm too scared to climb."

Owl Hooty?

She wanted to soar through the sky,

But as everyone knows, of course,

mouselings can't fly.

Batty Fangs?

　　He wanted to stay up till dawn,

But even the THOUGHT of it made Mouseling yawn.

She stared at the sky with her eyes big and wide.

Would she EVER find one who would stay by her side?

And as dark came in shadows and rain dropped in drips,
This mouseling ran out of her scurries and skips.

So she sat very quiet in her silvery fur –

No one seemed perfectly matching to her.

It seemed, in this world,
she was out on her own.
Deep in Wintermouse Wood
she felt . . .

quite alone.

But someone had heard her side-by-side song.

Someone who'd been around ALL ALONG.

He popped up his head from a very small hole –

A tinyful, weenimous, little black vole.

He was awfully quiet and terribly shy,

But he couldn't hear mouserly tears and stand by . . .

He peeped, "I'll be your friend!"

and he gave her a wink.

"Shall we dance ourselves happy?

What do you think?

We could make up some songs,"

he said, stroking his chin.

"Perhaps ALL of the wood

will want to join in!"

Oh! THIS was her other!

They'd make a great pair!

If only she'd noticed –

he'd always been there!

And now they had met

there was SO much to do.

They could do all the things

you can do as a TWO!

They could see-saw,

play catch

and sit back-to-back.

They could hide in their den and go halves on a snack.

They could sit and hold paws until daylight was gone.

Yes! Two little tails are much better than one.

They were peas in a pod, they were birds of a feather.

They were ALWAYS best friends – whatever the weather.

Two wonderful ones had found a forever,

And forever is great when you spend it together.

And now, side-by-side, they heard the same tune,

So they sung to the stars and they danced to the moon.

Yes, deep in the heart of
Wintermouse Wood,
A friend by your side
makes life twice as good.

For my side-by-siders. You make life double-wonderful – R.B

For near friends, far friends,
new friends, old friends and friends-to-be;
this one's for you with love – D.G

ORCHARD BOOKS
338 Euston Road, London NW1 3BH
Orchard Books Australia
Level 17/207 Kent Street, Sydney, NSW 2000
First published in 2015 by Orchard Books
ISBN 978 1 40833 161 3
Text © Rachel Bright 2015
Illustrations © Debi Gliori 2015
The rights of Rachel Bright to be identified as the author and Debi Gliori
to be identified as the illustrator of this work have been asserted by them in
accordance with the Copyright, Designs and Patents Act, 1988.
A CIP catalogue record for this book is available from the British Library.
1 3 5 7 9 10 8 6 4 2
Printed in China
Orchard Books is a division of Hachette Children's Books,
an Hachette UK company.
www.hachette.co.uk